★RICKY RICOTTA'S★

MIGHTY ROBOT

VS THE MUTANT MOSQUITOES FROM MERCURY

D0103968

from the creator of
CAPTAIN UNDERPANTS

another adventure novel by
Dav Pilkey
pictures
by **Martin Ontiveros**

SCHOLASTIC

Ricky Ricotta's Mighty Robot vs the Mutant Mosquitoes from Mercury

Ricky Ricotta's Mighty Robot vs the Mutant Mosquitoes from Mercury

The Second Robot Adventure Novel by
DAV PILKEY

Pictures by
MARTIN ONTIVEROS

■SCHOLASTIC

For Robbie Staenberg — D. P.

To Micki, Derek, Bwana, Marny,

Alicia, Craig, Kalah, JP,

and my cats — M. O.

Scholastic Children's Books,
Commonwealth House, 1-19 New Oxford Street,
London WC1A 1NU, UK
A division of Scholastic Ltd
London ~ New York ~ Toronto ~ Sydney ~ Auckland
Mexico City ~ New Delhi ~ Hong Kong

First published in the US by Scholastic Inc., 2000

First published in the UK by Scholastic Ltd, 2001

ISBN 0 439 99354 7
Printed and bound in Denmark by Nørhaven Paperback A/S
Reading, Berkshire
4 6 8 10 9 7 5

Chapters

CHAPTER 1

Ricky and His Robot

There once was a mouse called Ricky Ricotta who lived in Squeakyville with his mother and father.

Ricky Ricotta might have been
the smallest mouse around . . .

. . . but he had the BIGGEST
best friend in town.

CHAPTER 2

School Days

Ricky and his mighty Robot
liked to go to school together.

Sometimes, when Ricky
was running late, his Robot
would fly him straight to
the front door.

After school, the mighty Robot liked to help Ricky with his homework. The Robot's computer brain could solve complex maths problems . . .

$2 + 3 =$
5

. . . his finger had a built-in
pencil sharpener . . .

. . . and he could even remove his telescopic eyeball, which made studying the planets much easier.

"Wow," said Ricky. "I can see all
the way to Mercury! That's cool!"

CHAPTER 3

Mr Mosquito
Hates Mercury!

Mercury was the smallest planet
in the solar system, and it was
the closest planet to the sun. But
it certainly was not *cool*!

Just ask Mr Mosquito.
He lived on Mercury, and he
HATED everything about it!

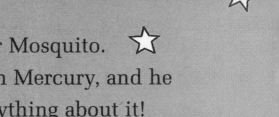

He hated the long, *long*, HOT days. Each day on Mercury, the temperature rose to more than four hundred degrees!

Mr Mosquito couldn't even walk down the street because his flip-flops always melted on the pavement.

Mr Mosquito hated Mercury's
long, *long*, COLD nights, too. Each
night on Mercury, the temperature
dropped to almost two hundred
degrees below zero!

Mr Mosquito couldn't even brush his teeth because his toothpaste was always frozen solid!

"I've g-g-got to g-g-get away f-f-from th-th-this awful p-p-planet," said Mr Mosquito, shivering in the cold. So Mr Mosquito looked through his telescope and saw the planet Earth.

He saw mice playing happily on cool autumn days.

He saw them sleeping soundly on warm summer nights.

"Earth is the planet for me!" said Mr Mosquito. "Soon it will be mine!"

CHAPTER 4

Mr Mosquito Makes His Move

Mr Mosquito went into his secret laboratory and clipped his filthy fingernails.

He put the clippings into
a giant machine and zapped
them with a powerful ray.

Then, Mr Mosquito's fingernails
grew and grew and grew . . .

. . . into massive Mutant Mosquitoes!

Mr Mosquito climbed aboard his spaceship and called to his troops.

"Mutant Mosquitoes," he cried, "it is time to conquer Earth! Follow me!"

And they did.

CHAPTER 5

The Mosquitoes Attack

When Mr Mosquito got to Earth,
he ordered his Mutant Mosquitoes
to attack Squeakyville.

Ricky was in his maths class
that afternoon. He looked out of
the window and saw the
Mutant Mosquitoes.

"Uh-oh," said Ricky. "It
looks like Squeakyville needs
our help!"

Ricky raised his hand.

"May I be excused?" Ricky asked his teacher. "My Robot and I have to save the Earth."

"Not until you've finished your maths test," said Ricky's teacher.

Ricky had three questions left. "What is two times three?" he asked himself aloud.

Ricky's Robot was waiting outside. He wanted to help. So he dashed to the teachers' car park and brought back some cars.

Ricky's Robot put three cars into one pile, and he put three cars into another pile.

Ricky looked at the piles of cars.
"*Two* piles of *three* cars," said
Ricky. "Two times three equals *six*!"

Ricky looked at his next question.
"What is *six* minus *five*?" he asked.
Ricky's Robot knew just what to do.

He threw five of the cars back
into the car park.

"I get it," said Ricky. "Six
minus five equals *one*!"

Ricky's last question was the
hardest of all.

"What is *one* divided by *two*?"
he asked.

The Robot used his mighty karate chop to divide one car in two.

"That was easy," said Ricky. "One divided by two equals *one-half*!"

Ricky handed in his test. Then he climbed out of the window.

"Let's go, mighty Robot," said Ricky. "We've got to save the Earth."

"M-m-m-my *car*!" cried Ricky's teacher.

CHAPTER 6

The Heroes Arrive

Ricky and his mighty Robot ran to the city centre to face the Mutant Mosquitoes.

The Mosquitoes attacked
Ricky's Robot.

"Hey," said Ricky. "Four
against one is not fair!"

Then Ricky had an idea.

"Come with me, Robot," said Ricky.

The mighty Robot was busy
fighting, so he could not follow
Ricky. But his arm could stretch
very far!

Ricky and his Robot's arm stretched all the way to the "Bugs Away" bug-spray factory.

Ricky told the Robot's arm to grab one of the huge bug-spray storage tanks.

Then they headed back to the battle.

CHAPTER 7

A Buggy Battle

The Robot shook the
tank of bug spray.

The Robot sprayed the Mosquitoes.

Then he broke up the buggy battle with a big blast from his bionic boot!

CHAPTER 8

Mr Mosquito's Revenge

The Mutant Mosquitoes had been defeated. Ricky's mighty Robot chased them into space.

The Mosquitoes flew back to
Mercury and never bothered
anybody again.

Mr Mosquito was very angry.
He grabbed Ricky and took
him into his spaceship. "Help
me, Robot," Ricky cried.

But it was too late. Mr Mosquito
chained Ricky up. Then he went to
his control panel and pulled a
secret lever.

Suddenly his spaceship began
to change. It shifted . . .

. . . and grew . . .

. . . and transformed into a giant
Mecha-Mosquito!

The Mecha-Mosquito attacked
Ricky's mighty Robot. But Ricky's
Robot would not fight back.

He knew that Ricky was inside
the Mecha-Mosquito, and he did
not want his best friend to get hurt.

The Mecha-Mosquito
pounded Ricky's Robot.

What could Ricky do?

Ricky thought and thought.

Then he had an idea.

"Mr Mosquito," said Ricky,
"I have to go to the toilet."

"Not now," said Mr Mosquito.
"I am too busy beating up
your Robot!"

"But it's an emergency,"
said Ricky.

"All right, all right," said Mr
Mosquito. He unlocked Ricky's
chains and led him to the boys'
toilets.

"Hurry up in there!" he yelled.

Inside the bathroom, Ricky opened a window and stuck his head outside.

"Pssssst!" Ricky whispered.

The Robot saw Ricky, and
he held out his giant hand.

Ricky jumped.

"I'm safe," said Ricky.

"Now it will be a fair fight!"

CHAPTER 9

Ricky's Robot Strikes Back

Inside the Mecha-Mosquito, Mr Mosquito was getting very angry. He knocked on the toilet door. "Let's hurry up in there!" he yelled. "I haven't got all da—"

KER-POW!

Ricky's Robot punched the
Mecha-Mosquito right in the face.

Mr Mosquito leaped to his
control panel and fought back hard.
The final battle was about to begin.

CHAPTER 10

The Final Battle

(IN FLIP-O-RAMA™)

D-RAMA

HERE'S HOW IT WORKS!

STEP 1
Place your *left* hand inside the dotted lines marked "LEFT HAND HERE". Hold the book open *flat*.

STEP 2
Grasp the *right-hand* page with your right thumb and index finger (inside the dotted lines marked "RIGHT THUMB HERE").

STEP 3
Now *quickly* flip the right-hand page back and forth until the picture appears to be *animated*.

(For extra fun, try adding your own sound effects!)

FLIP-O-RAMA 1

(pages 85 and 87)

Remember, flip *only* page 85.
While you are flipping, make sure
you can see the picture on page 85
and the one on page 87.
If you flip quickly, the two
pictures will start to look like
<u>one</u> *animated* picture.

Don't forget to add
your own sound effects!

LEFT HAND HERE

The Mecha-Mosquito Attacked.

RIGHT THUMB HERE

The Mecha-Mosquito
Attacked.

FLIP-O-RAMA 2

(pages 89 and 91)

Remember, flip *only* page 89.
While you are flipping, make sure
you can see the picture on page 89
and the one on page 91.
If you flip quickly, the two
pictures will start to look like
<u>one</u> *animated* picture.

Don't forget to add
your own sound effects!

LEFT HAND HERE

Ricky's Robot
Fought Back.

89

RIGHT
THUMB
HERE

90

Ricky's Robot
Fought Back.

FLIP-O-RAMA 3

(pages 93 and 95)

Remember, flip *only* page 93.
While you are flipping, make sure
you can see the picture on page 93
and the one on page 95.
If you flip quickly, the two
pictures will start to look like
<u>one</u> *animated* picture.

Don't forget to add
your own sound effects!

LEFT HAND HERE

The Mecha-Mosquito
Battled Hard.

RIGHT
THUMB
HERE

The Mecha-Mosquito
Battled Hard.

FLIP-O-RAMA 4

(pages 97 and 99)

Remember, flip *only* page 97.
While you are flipping, make sure
you can see the picture on page 97
and the one on page 99.
If you flip quickly, the two
pictures will start to look like
<u>one</u> *animated* picture.

Don't forget to add
your own sound effects!

LEFT HAND HERE

Ricky's Robot
Battled Harder.

97

RIGHT
THUMB
HERE

Ricky's Robot
Battled Harder.

FLIP-O-RAMA 5

(pages 101 and 103)

Remember, flip *only* page 101.
While you are flipping, make sure
you can see the picture on page 101
and the one on page 103.
If you flip quickly, the two
pictures will start to look like
<u>one</u> *animated* picture.

Don't forget to add
your own sound effects!

LEFT HAND HERE

Ricky's Robot
Saved the Day!

101

RIGHT
THUMB
HERE

RIGHT
INDEX
FINGER
HERE

Ricky's Robot
Saved the Day!

CHAPTER 11

Justice Prevails

The Mecha-Mosquito
had been destroyed, and
Ricky Ricotta's mighty Robot
was victorious.

Mr Mosquito crawled out of his damaged ship and began to cry. "What a bad day I am having," cried Mr Mosquito.

"It's about to get worse," said Ricky.

Ricky's mighty Robot picked up
Mr Mosquito and dropped him
into the Squeakyville prison.

Then Ricky and his mighty Robot
flew home for chocolate milk and
grilled cheese sandwiches.

"You boys have saved the world again," said Ricky's mother.

"Yes," said Ricky's father.
"Thank you for sticking together
and fighting for what was right!"
"No problem," said Ricky . . .

"that's what friends are for."

HOW TO DRAW RICKY

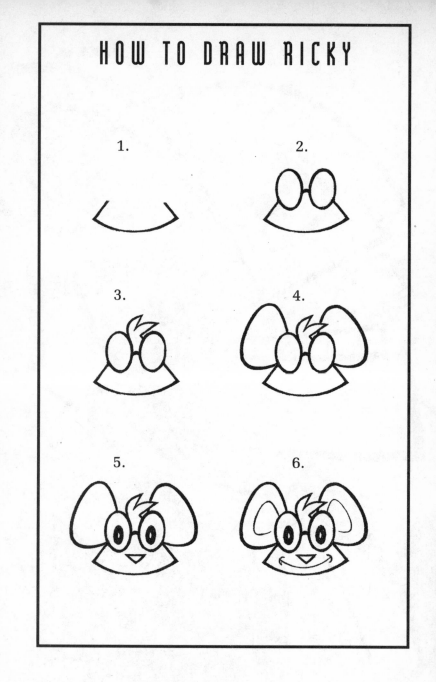

1.

2.

3.

4.

5.

6.

1.

2.

3.

4.

5.

6.

HOW TO DRAW RICKY'S ROBOT

1.

2.

3.

4.

6.

7.

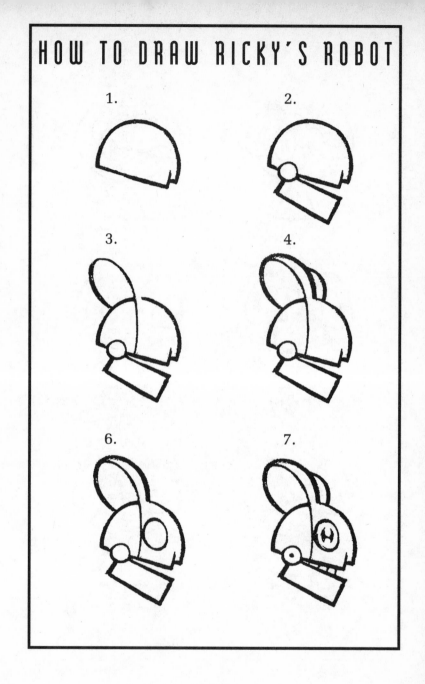

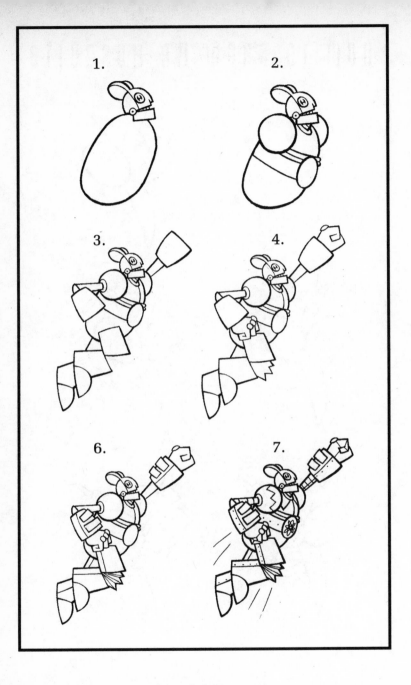

1.

2.

3.

4.

6.

7.

HOW TO DRAW MR MOSQUITO

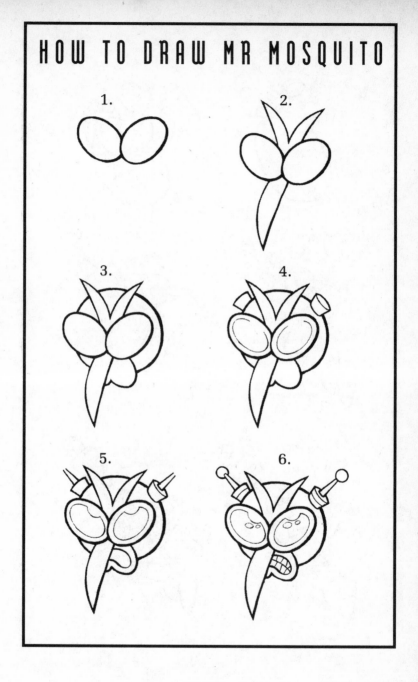

1.

2.

3.

4.

5.

6.

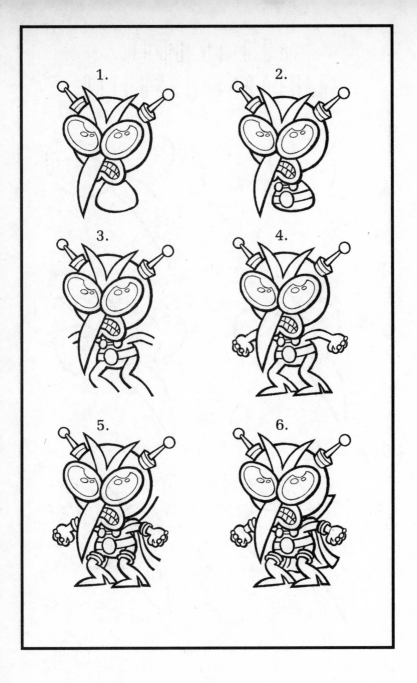

HOW TO DRAW
A MUTANT MOSQUITO

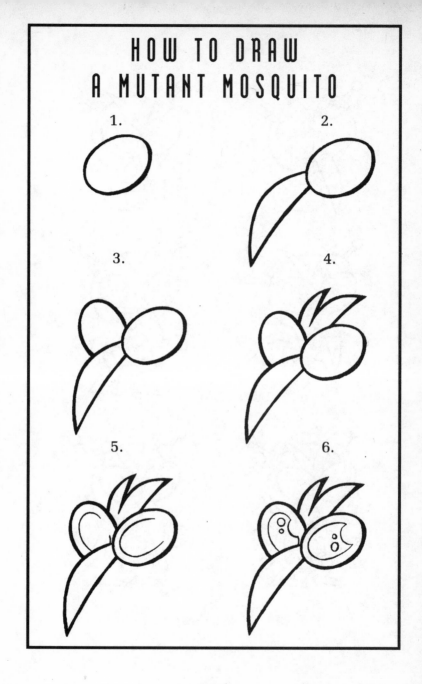

HOLD ON TO YOUR
SEATS, KIDS!

Ricky Ricotta's next adventure will be to battle the Voodoo Vultures from Venus!

COMING SOON:

Ricky Ricotta's Mighty Robot

vs

The Voodoo Vultures from Venus

The Mecha-Monkeys from Mars

The Jurassic Jack Rabbits from Jupiter

The Stupid Stinkbugs from Saturn

The Uranium Unicorns from Uranus

The Naughty Night Crawlers from Neptune

The Un-Pleasant Penguins from Pluto

About the Author and Illustrator

DAV PILKEY created his first stories as comic books while he was in elementary school. In 1997, he wrote and illustrated his first adventure novel for children, *The Adventures of Captain Underpants*, which received rave reviews and was an instant best-seller — as were the other books that followed in the series. Dav is also the creator of numerous award-winning picture books. He and his dog live in Seattle, Washington.

It was a stroke of luck when Dav discovered the work of artist **MARTIN ONTIVEROS**. Dav knew that Martin was just the right illustrator for the Ricky Ricotta's Mighty Robot series. Martin lives in Portland, Oregon. He has a lot of toys as well as two cats, Bunny and Spanky.

Visit Dav Pilkey's Extra-Crunchy
Web Site O'Fun at:
www.pilkey.com